PERFECT MAN

To Nana, Pop, Grandma, Grandpa, and every other
superhero I've ever known, retired or otherwise.
And to Roger Stern and Joseph Torchia,
for their own obsessive boys.
T.W.

For Perfect Man, who cleverly disguised himself as
Mr. Heise and Mr. Brewer—two brilliant teachers.
D.G.

Text copyright © 2004 Troy Wilson

Illustrations copyright © 2004 Dean Griffiths

National Library of Canada Cataloguing in Publication Data

Wilson, Troy, 1970-
Perfect man / story by Troy Wilson ; illustrations by Dean Griffiths.

ISBN 1-55143-286-2

I. Griffiths, Dean, 1967- II. Title.

PS8645.I47P47 2004   jC813'.6   C2003-907398-X

First published in the United States 2004

Library of Congress Control Number: 2003116363

Summary: Michael's superhero abandons him, leaving him to discover
his own super powers with the help of a wonderful teacher.

Orca Book Publishers gratefully acknowledges the support of its publishing program
provided by the following agencies: the Department of Canadian Heritage,
the Canada Council for the Arts, and the British Columbia Arts Council.

Design by Lynn O'Rourke
Printed and bound in Hong Kong

Orca Book Publishers
1030 North Park Street
Victoria, BC Canada
V8T 1C6

Orca Book Publishers
PO Box 468
Custer, WA   USA
98240-0468

07 06 05 04 • 4 3 2 1

PERFECT MAN

Story by Troy Wilson
Illustrations by Dean Griffiths

ORCA BOOK PUBLISHERS

Michael Maxwell McAllum was the smallest boy in his class. He lived in a small house in a small town on a small street. Sometimes he went on trips with his family.

Perfect Man was the greatest superhero of them all. He lived... well... no one knows where he lived. Sometimes he went to other dimensions.

Michael Maxwell McAllum was Perfect Man's biggest fan.

He covered his walls with Perfect Man posters. He read Perfect Man comics and played Perfect Man video games. He ate Perfect Man cereal and wore Perfect Man T-shirts.

He watched Perfect Man on the six o'clock news. He cut Perfect Man out of the newspaper. He wrote Perfect Man stories. He made a Perfect Man website.

Before he went to sleep each night, he turned
out his Perfect Man lamp. He dreamed about
Perfect Man.

Perfect Man,

Perfect Man,

Perfect Man.

And then Perfect Man quit.

Just like that. He said it was time for a change.
He said it was time to start a new chapter in his life.

"Who will save the world when you're gone?" the
reporters asked.

"I used to be the only superhero around,"
Perfect Man said. "These days, it's hard to keep
track of them all. They'll do just fine without me."

"What's your secret identity?"

Perfect Man smiled. "If I told you, it wouldn't be
much of a secret, would it?"

"Where will you go?"

"Someplace quiet," Perfect Man said.

"What will you do?"

"You must be so sad," Michael's mother said. "You must feel like you've lost your best friend."

She didn't understand. She didn't know Perfect Man like he did. Perfect Man would come back. Just like the time he came back from deep space when he escaped the cosmic pirates. Just like the time he came back from Dimension Z when he beat Zrog the Unbeatable. Just like the time he came back from the dead when he... well... died. He *always* came back. Always.

That summer, Michael Maxwell McAllum watched on TV as aliens invaded New York.

They always invaded New York. They never invaded his small town. The Amazing Five teamed up with the Super Squadron to stop them.

Perfect Man will come back, he thought.

Summer ended.

Michael Maxwell McAllum went back to school.

And Perfect Man came back. Just like that. Perfect Man had changed. Michael didn't recognize him at first. He wasn't wearing his costume anymore. His hair was thinner. His stomach was rounder. He didn't even call himself Perfect Man anymore. He called himself Mr. Clark.

He was Michael Maxwell McAllum's new teacher.

Mr. Clark never broke the chalk. He never lost his temper. And he never got sick.

When Mr. Clark talked about the planets, it seemed as if he had visited them himself.

When there was trouble in the schoolyard, Mr. Clark was there. When Alexander dropped his art project, Mr. Clark was there. He was everywhere at once. At least it seemed that way.

Mr. Clark was the fastest marker in the world. And, best of all, Mr. Clark looked inside people. He saw all the good stuff and helped them bring it out. He helped them find their super powers.

Michael Maxwell McAllum knew Mr. Clark was Perfect Man. He was sure of it. But he didn't post it on his website. He didn't tell Mom or Dad. He didn't tell anybody. Instead, he wrote a story about Perfect Man. In the story, Perfect Man became a teacher in a small town. Only one boy suspected his secret. When Perfect Man decided to fight crime again, he made the boy his sidekick.

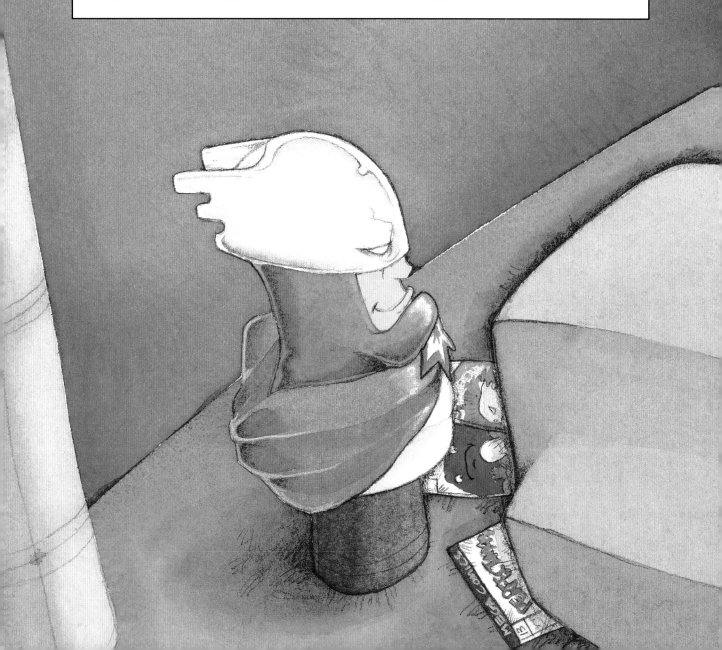

Michael Maxwell McAllum gave the story to Mr. Clark.

"Well, that's an original story," Mr. Clark said. "It's the best Perfect Man story you've written yet. I think the ending could use a little work, though."

"I know you're Perfect Man," Michael said.

Mr. Clark smiled. "Do I look like Perfect Man?"

"You're disguised," Michael answered. "I remember how you kept Dr. Plasma's shape-changing machine when he went to jail. Or maybe your friend the Dark Avenger helped you out. He's a master of disguises."

"Those are good theories," said Mr. Clark.

"Am I right?" asked Michael.

Mr. Clark didn't say "yes" and he didn't say "no." He said, "If Perfect Man were here today, he'd tell you exactly what I'm telling you now. You don't need to be the sidekick, Michael. You can be the superhero."

"What do you mean?" asked Michael.

"You already have a super power," said Mr. Clark. "You have the power to write. You write very well."

"I guess I write okay ... "

"No," Mr. Clark insisted. "You write very well. Do you like to write?"

Michael nodded.

"Then I hope you keep writing," said Mr. Clark. "I really do."

He paused. "Do you want to know a secret, Michael?"

Michael Maxwell McAllum leaned forward. "Yes. Yes, I do."

"To be a good writer, you have to read and you have to write," said Mr. Clark. "But there's another step. A secret step."

"What?" asked Michael. "What is it?"

"You have to live," said Mr. Clark. "You have to try new things. You have to meet new people. That's what good writers do. They live. And it's all research. Every second of it."

Michael leaned back. He thought for a second. Then he said, "I have one question."

"Yes?"

"What does flying feel like?"

Mr. Clark laughed. "Don't you have another story to write?" he said.

Michael Maxwell McAllum did have another story to write. He had a lot of other stories to write. Some of them were wonderful. Some of them were awful. And most of them were somewhere in between.

He tried new things and met new friends. He made new mistakes.

"It's research," he told himself over and over again. "It's all research."

He grew and he wrote and he lived.

Today Mr. Clark is still a teacher. He loves what he does. Sometimes he thinks about Perfect Man and smiles.

Michael Maxwell McAllum is a best-selling author. He loves what he does.

MICHAEL M
MICHAEL M McALLUM
PERFECT MAN
MICHAEL M McALLUM
PERFECT MAN
PERFECT MAN
ORIGINS

Mr. Clark is Michael Maxwell McAllum's biggest fan.